THE LOCHSIDE MURDER

A DORS

RACHEL MCLEAN

ACKROYD
PUBLISHING

Copyright © 2023 by Rachel McLean

All rights reserved.

No part of this book may be reproduced in any form or by any electronic or mechanical means, including information storage and retrieval systems, without written permission from the author, except for the use of brief quotations in a book review.

This is a work of fiction. Names, characters, businesses, places, events and incidents are either the products of the author's imagination or used in a fictitious manner. Any resemblance to actual persons, living or dead, or actual events is purely coincidental.

Ackroyd Publishing

ackroyd-publishing.com

THE LOCHSIDE MURDER

CHAPTER ONE

THE ROOM WAS dark when DCI Lesley Clarke woke up, and for a moment she wondered where she was.

She lay back on the pillows, listening. The flat she and Elsa shared in Bournemouth was quiet in the mornings, the only sound the seagulls screeching over the beach three streets away.

But the bed was at the wrong angle. She could see light seeping round curtains and it was at the side of the bed, not the foot.

She remembered, smiling. Rolling over, she snuggled up to Elsa.

"Morning, Mrs Clarke."

Elsa grunted and turned over. There was no *Morning, Mrs Short* in return.

Lesley rolled onto her back and stared up into the darkness. They'd arrived late the previous night, picking their way down a path lit only by dim wall-mounted lanterns and convincing themselves that the vague reflections they could see and the quiet swish they could hear meant that Loch

Lomond really was right in front of their cabin. In the dark, it was difficult to tell.

She reached over to the bedside table and picked up her phone. 6.45 am. Her subconscious was insistent on reminding her it was a work day.

She yawned.

Go back to sleep, woman.

But she was wide awake. And she wanted to check the view beyond those curtains.

She slid out of bed, careful not to wake the now-snoring Elsa, and padded to the stairs leading from their mezzanine bedroom to the open plan living room below. She'd hauled their cases up those stairs last night; there was no way she was forgetting the layout.

At the bottom of the stairs, Lesley paused. The windows spanned almost the entire front wall of the cabin, so close to the loch they might as well have been in a boat.

She walked to the nearest window and leaned her forehead against the glass. It was cool, but not as chilly as she'd been expecting.

But out there, it would be freezing. March in Scotland? Ice blocks.

Yawning, she flicked the coffee maker on and inserted a pod. Five minutes later she was back at the window, watching birds skim across the water and clouds scud over the mountains beyond the opposite bank.

It was beautiful.

She checked her phone again – still not seven o'clock. She had a good hour before Elsa would stir.

She went to the rucksack by the front door and pulled out her fleece, hat and gloves. She crept back upstairs and grabbed her jeans from a chair, then crept downstairs to pull them on over her pyjamas.

Her thickest winter coat, the one she'd bought after her first case in Dorset had made it clear that practical clothes would be the order of the day, was on a hook by the door. She shrugged it on, turned the key in the lock and stepped outside.

My God, it was cold.

She tugged on her gloves and pulled her hat further down her head, wishing she'd brought a second one. She zipped up the coat and batted her hands together to try and inject some warmth into her arms.

Get moving. That would warm her up.

The only way along the loch side – or anywhere, really – was back up the narrow path they'd come down last night, through a gate and along another path leading past two other holiday homes to the south. To her right, past some trees, was the A82. Elsa had driven along it the night before, headlights appearing intermittently from the opposite direction and blinding them. It was a fast road, but a quiet one. The worst kind.

Beyond the holiday homes, she found a path leading along the banks of the loch. This was better. She picked up her pace, feeling the blood return to her extremities, and hummed under her breath.

The Wedding March.

She smiled. They hadn't even played that, but it had been stuck in her head for days now. Days during which she'd been busy solving the murder of a local criminal, and worrying her new wife might have something to do with it.

She'd stopped worrying now. Elsa had promised to have nothing to do with the Kelvin family from now on, and they couldn't exactly forge a life together if Lesley wasn't prepared to believe her.

After five minutes of walking, she came to a bend in the path leading inland and around another group of houses. More holiday properties. No actual homes along here, it seemed. It reminded her of parts of Dorset. Bustling in the summer, deserted in the winter.

She liked the winter months. At least she could get to a crime scene in under an hour, and didn't have to fight her way past the queue to use the Sandbanks ferry.

She rounded the houses and followed the path back to the water's edge. It led to the back door of one of the properties, but there was no sign of occupation. Besides: this was Scotland. Wasn't there a right to roam?

There was a small shingle beach next to the house. It would give her a great view.

But as she neared the water, she smelt something that made her stop in her tracks.

Lesley sniffed again, then stopped herself, wishing she could close her nostrils.

She knew that smell.

Shit.

I'm on bloody holiday.

She should turn back.

Turn around and go back to her wife. Forget all about it.

But any responsible member of the public would investigate further. Make a call.

She didn't have to be a copper. She could just be a civic-minded passer-by.

She picked her way over the shingle towards a jetty that led out over the water. There was a shape under the jetty, partially but not completely obscured.

Lesley's stomach lurched.

She put a hand to her mouth.

Dear God. Poor bastard.

The body was on its back, legs splayed into the water. It wore what looked like red trousers and a brown jacket.

It was wedged under the jetty, jammed there in a way that prevented the body from moving with the currents in the water.

It wasn't clear if it was a man or woman, young or old. Mainly because the face had been all but destroyed.

Lesley turned away and took a breath.

OK. She took another breath. *Make the call. Don't get involved.*

Police Scotland would sort it out.

Wouldn't they?

Of course they would.

She'd brought her phone with her, in case Elsa woke. She turned away from the body, pushed out a juddering breath, and dialled.

CHAPTER TWO

"You OK, BOSS? YOU LOOK PENSIVE."

DI Jade Tanner looked up from her phone at DS Mo Uddin, her second-in-command. She'd been trawling the Police Scotland website for vacancies.

Not that she was about to tell Mo that. The poor sod had only bought a house in Stirling six weeks ago, moved his kids up here. Jade didn't want him knowing their unit might be at risk.

"I'm fine, Mo. You got that report into historic gun crime in Glasgow for me?"

His nose twitched. "I have. You sure this is the kind of thing we should be focusing on?"

"We haven't been allocated a case for two months. We need to keep busy."

"And justify our existence."

She looked at him. "Since when were you so cynical?"

"Since I saw you looking at job vacancies."

Jade slammed her laptop screen shut. "You weren't s'posed to see that."

"Sorry."

She leaned back in her chair. It was early; the other two members of the team, Stuart and Patty, weren't in yet. And their part-time freelance advisor Petra McBride hadn't darkened their doors in months. She was probably halfway round the world on a glamorous case. Or chasing romance.

"D'you really think the Complex Crimes Unit could get closed down?" Mo asked. "Has Detective Superintendent Murdo said something?"

Fraser had said nothing. Nothing about the unit being closed down, anyway. But no matter how hard he tried, local CID units weren't referring cases to them. No matter how complex.

Jade's phone rang. *The very woman.*

"Dr McBride," Jade said, "how's things?"

"Now now, don't be so formal, lass."

"Sorry, Petra. I hope you're busier than we are."

At least Jade, Mo, Patty and Stuart were still being paid to do nothing. Petra, as a freelancer, needed to keep busy.

"I do alright, Jade. I do alright."

"Tell me you've called with the case that's going to make our reputation and ensure the future of the CCU."

A laugh. "Can't do that, sorry. I just wanted to check you wouldn't be needing me for the next month."

Jade spotted Mo watching her. She mouthed *Petra* and he nodded and returned to his screen.

"Not that I know of," she told the doctor. "Why d'you ask?"

"I've been offered some work in France."

"Alright for some."

"I wouldn't speak too soon. I'm to interview a terrorist suspect, get to grips with his psychology."

Jade shuddered. "Tell me there'll be plenty of croissants and beef bourguignon to make up for it."

Petra chuckled. "I'll make sure of that. Anyway before I take this job, I wanted to be sure you wouldn't be needing me."

"That's kind of you, Petra, but you don't need to prioritise us. I'm sure France is a lot more glamourous."

"I'm not prioritising you, hen. I'd rather stay local, just for now."

"Oh yes?" Jade knew Petra well enough to understand that this meant there was a new girlfriend on the scene, and that she was Scottish.

"Don't get excited. Early days yet. But if you've nothing for me, I'll be off to Paris on Friday."

"This Friday coming?"

"Five days away, yes. There a problem with that?"

"No. You have a lovely time."

Jade sighed. Truth was, she was jealous.

"I will," Petra replied. "Keep in touch if you've work for me, yes?"

"Will do." Jade hung up.

Mo had his phone to his ear. He was frowning, his hand cupped over the mouthpiece. Jade tried to catch his eye but he was too focused on the call.

A case, she hoped. But those didn't come in via the DS. That wasn't the way things were done.

The office door opened and Patty strode in, bringing cold air with her.

"Shut the door!" Jade called. They worked in an open plan office on a business estate, in a building designed for many more people than just the four of them. It was permanently freezing, even in summer. Especially at the end of a winter that just didn't want to end.

"Sorry, boss." Patty turned and pushed the door firmly closed. "Any new cases?"

"Nope," said Jade.

"Yes." Mo had finished his call and was holding his phone in both hands.

"That was a case?" Jade asked, gesturing at his phone.

"That was my old boss."

"Zoe?" Jade felt her chest grow heavy. "She's recalling you."

Mo shook his head, his eyes alight. "Not Zoe. DCI Clarke, her old boss. She's on honeymoon at Loch Lomond, and she's found a body."

CHAPTER THREE

"Elsa, wake up." Lesley bent over the bed, her hand on Elsa's shoulder.

"What?" Elsa opened her eyes then closed them again. "Turn it off." She reached for a light switch, not finding one.

"Sorry, sweetie," Lesley said. "But something's happened."

Elsa sat up in bed. Lesley had partially opened the curtains and turned on the bathroom light, leaving the door open.

"Is it Sharon?" Elsa asked, her voice thick with sleep. "Is she OK?"

"It's not Sharon." Lesley's teenage daughter was with her dad in Birmingham; she'd be fine.

Elsa's shoulders slumped. "Please don't tell me it's work. You promised me you wouldn't pick up work calls while we were here."

"And I haven't. I won't."

Lesley had had four calls from Stanley and one from Tina since leaving for Scotland. She'd ignored them all. And her team knew better than to leave voicemails when she was on holiday.

Dennis was in charge. He could deal with it. And if not Dennis, DI Varney, who was still seconded to their team after their latest murder case.

"So what, then?" Elsa ran a hand through her long dark hair. It was tangled.

"I'm sorry, love." Lesley sat on the bed next to her, curling her feet beneath her. "I found something."

"I don't get it." Elsa rubbed her eyes. "Where's my water?" She reached for the bedside table and grabbed a glass. She gulped half of it down and smacked her lips together.

She looked into Lesley's eyes.

"Please, tell me this isn't work."

"It isn't. Well, not really."

Elsa sighed. "I don't know what 'not really' means, but you promised me—"

Lesley put a finger to her wife's lips. "You were asleep and I wanted to see the views, so I went for a walk. And I found a body."

"A body? What sort of body?"

"A dead one. Is there any other kind?"

"You found a dead body, just by coincidence? You're sure you didn't work your way onto a local murder case?"

Lesley shook her head. "There *will* be a local murder case, now. But no. I'm the proverbial dog-walker. I was out minding my own business and I came upon a dead body."

Elsa pulled back the duvet and swung her feet out of the bed. "Where are my slippers?"

Lesley grabbed the slippers that had come with the cabin and put them next to Elsa's feet.

"Thanks." Elsa stood up and made for the stairs. "I don't understand."

Lesley followed her down. "It was an IC1 female, not sure what age. She was wearing red trousers and a tweedy jacket when she died. Her arms showed signs of a struggle and despite her legs being in the loch, I don't think she drowned. But the main thing—"

They were at the bottom of the stairs. Elsa turned to Lesley. "Stop right there. Can you hear yourself?"

"I was just a passer-by."

"What kind of passer-by looks for signs of a struggle and identifies the ethnicity of the victim? You report it, and you bugger off sharpish."

"I did report it."

"Good. So we can get on with our honeymoon." Elsa flicked the kettle on. "I'm going to make a pot of tea, then we can go for a walk. Or a pub lunch. There's that place we saw on the—"

"Elsa."

Elsa was opening cupboards, looking for a mug. "What?" Her voice had darkened.

"It's not as simple as that."

"You're not investigating this death, if that's what you mean."

Lesley put a hand on Elsa's arm. "No. But I will need to make a statement. Police Scotland will want to talk to me."

"When?" Elsa poured hot water into a mug.

"I'm not sure. We'd probably best not go for that pub lunch."

Elsa's face creased. "Lesley love, I was looking forward to some normality. We've only got five days here. Just call 999, and leave it alone."

"I made the call, I told you. I'll give Mo my statement and then we can enjoy ourselves."

"Mo? Who's Mo?"

Lesley felt her face redden. "DS Mo Uddin. He used to work for me in Birmingham."

Elsa sipped her tea. She eyed Lesley over the rim of her mug. "Don't tell me, he's stationed up here now."

Lesley nodded. "Complex Crimes Unit. They're on their way."

Elsa slumped into a chair. "This isn't fair, Lesley. This is going to ruin our honeymoon."

CHAPTER FOUR

JADE LOOKED on as the CSIs roped crime scene tape around the jetty, two uniformed officers helping them. She took in the scene.

To her left was what looked like a holiday home. There was no car parked in the drive, and no one had answered when Patty knocked. And when she'd looked through the kitchen window, she'd seen no sign of personalisation or recent habitation.

It was March in Scotland. Of course the holiday homes were empty. Even this close to the water.

To the left of the jetty was a small shingle beach and beyond that, a footpath. The path led through some woods, into the grounds of a hotel and then on to Balloch.

Leading down to the jetty was a road. They'd cordoned it off as far as the slip road from the A82, in the hope of finding tyre tracks.

Whoever had left the body here had probably come in a vehicle and attempted to use the jetty to dump it in the water.

Instead, the currents had washed it back in and it had got stuck. She wondered if the killer had hung around for long enough to know that had happened. If they'd tried to dislodge the body but decided to stop for fear of leaving more evidence.

One thing was for sure: they definitely had a murder case on their hands. And one that merited the Complex Crimes Unit. The face was a mess, the bones caved in. There were marks where a weapon had been used. It certainly didn't look like an accident.

She could just about make out the bloodied face from here, but it wasn't clear. Forensics were keeping people as far away from the scene as possible.

Identifying the body would be made harder by its state, but not impossible. She was waiting to hear if the fingers were still intact. And there was the hope of being able to match the DNA or teeth with records from Mispers. It was a long shot, but it was worth a go.

All the sort of thing the local police would have managed, in truth. It was possible, she supposed, that the only thing making this a complex crime was the fact that Mo's old boss had called it in to them. If it hadn't been for that, they might not have had a sniff.

Jamie Douglas, the Crime Scene Manager, was standing near the jetty, overseeing the taping. He turned and approached Jade.

"DI Tanner."

"Jamie. What have we got?"

"No sign of blood. Tyre tracks leading to the jetty, multiple sets so it's not going to be easy finding a match."

"Nothing in the water?"

"There're divers booked in. They'll be here this afternoon."

Jade jiggled her feet. It was cold out here by the water. Her own home was just four miles north, right on the banks of the loch. But she rarely opened the windows at this time of year, and certainly didn't set foot outside if she could help it.

That had been Dan's thing. Out there on the deck, watching the birds, unaffected by the cold.

She'd taken him mugs of coffee, scarves and extra coats. Each time he'd shrugged them away, irritated that she might disturb the wildlife.

And now that deck was empty.

"Boss." Patty was looking over her shoulder, back towards the road. "We've got an observer."

Jade turned to see a woman standing near the road. She wore a coat that was too big for her, along with jeans and muddy walking boots. She had blonde hair and a deep frown on her face.

"She a local?" Patty asked, knowing Jade lived nearby.

"Never seen her before."

"She's the one who found the body," Jamie said. "She was here earlier."

Mo's old boss. Jade wondered what she would be like. If she'd been a factor in him moving up here.

But she'd moved away from Birmingham before him, hadn't she? Somewhere down south. Jade wasn't sure where.

"OK," she said. "I'll have a word with her. Patty, you stay here, let me know if anything else turns up. Are Uniform doing a trawl of the banks along from here?"

"They're on their way," Jamie told her. "Nearest station is Helensburgh, only a couple of guys there. The rest of them'll have to come from Dumbarton, Glasgow too. I'll get them looking south of here to start with. That's where the current is leading. What there is of it."

"Thanks." Jade gave him a smile and approached the woman. She was standing very still, her movements barely noticeable. She'd picked a spot on a clean area of tarmac. Preserving the scene.

Jade held out a hand as she approached the woman. "DCI Clarke? I'm DI Jade Tanner."

The woman gave her a smile. It was genuine enough, but didn't feel entirely heartfelt. "Lesley. I found the body."

"You used to manage my DS."

"Well, I managed his DI. But yes. He's a good detective. You're lucky to have him."

Jade nodded. She'd seen hints of Mo's ability, but the truth was he'd had little opportunity to make use of it.

"What time was it you found the body?" she asked.

Lesley blinked and then scratched her cheek as if coming to. "Seven thirty-four. I'm staying in a cabin along the way" – she indicated – "with my wife. I woke up early and wanted to get a look at the loch."

"Did you notice it from a distance, or were you already on it when you spotted it?"

"If you're asking to what degree I've dirtied your crime scene, then not much. I took pains to retreat via my original footsteps. Your CSM down there has already taken prints of my boots." She lifted her foot to show traces of ink on the heels. "And I'll let you have a DNA sample if you need it."

"Thanks. Was there anyone else in the vicinity?"

"You're wondering if I saw the bastard who dumped her here."

"You know it's a woman."

"I got a good enough look. And I heard your DC talking to the Forensics guys. You got an ID yet?"

"I'm sorry, Ma'am, but I'm going to have to bring you back to the question. Did you see anyone else in the vicinity? Any cars leaving? Anyone on foot?"

The woman got out her phone. "There was a silver Aygo parked up on the roadway there." She pointed. "You want the plate?"

Jade smiled. If you had to have an outsider finding a body, it was probably a good thing that outsider was a police-woman on holiday. "Please."

The DCI rattled off a registration number.

"Anything else? Anyone in the car?"

"Not that I noticed. I wasn't looking when I arrived, and by the time I'd seen the body and walked back to the road, the car was leaving."

"You couldn't tell how many people were in it."

"Sorry."

Jade put her notebook into her pocket. "Thanks for noting the plates though. I'm sure it's a coincidence."

"You can't assume anything." The DCI gave her a look. Jade met her gaze. This woman might be her senior, but she was on holiday and from an entirely different force.

"So you didn't see anyone on foot."

"Nobody."

"And when you found the body...?"

"I didn't spot it until I was almost on it. I couldn't tell that the head was that badly damaged from the angle of approach. I saw the legs first, then walked carefully to the jetty, making sure to leave as few prints as possible. I'm sure you'll under-stand I thought it might have been a situation in which I could have helped someone who'd collapsed or got into trouble in the water."

"Wearing winter clothing."

The DCI shrugged. "You never know."

No. "Did you touch the body at all?"

"DI Tanner, I'm not an idiot. As soon as I realised the individual was dead, I moved away. As I've told you, I was careful not to disturb the scene. But no, I didn't touch it. Or anything else."

"You're sure you didn't touch anything on your approach?"

"I can't be a hundred percent, but no, my instincts meant I was cautious. There's not much I can help you with, I'm afraid."

"Thank you for what you have done."

The DCI nodded again. "You didn't bring DS Uddin to the scene."

"He's nearby, with Uniform. Knocking on doors, finding out if anyone's gone missing. We're anxious to get an ID as quickly as—"

"Of course you are. Well, if I can help at all..." The woman checked her watch. "I need to get back."

"If you'll let me have your address, so we can take a formal statement."

"Of course." The DCI gave her the address of a set of holiday cottages less than half a mile away. Jade knew them well; Dan's parents had stayed in one of them when they'd visited.

"Thanks, DCI Clarke."

"My pleasure."

The woman walked away, towards the road. Jade

wondered if she went looking for trouble when she was on holiday, or if it just came to her.

Once a copper, always a copper.

She sniffed and headed back towards the jetty. Hopefully they'd find something to help them identify the victim, and soon.

CHAPTER FIVE

DOOR-TO-DOOR along the shores of Loch Lomond was significantly different to door-to-door back in Birmingham.

For starters, the transition between houses meant getting back in the car most times, rather than walking down a footpath or driveway, along a few feet of pavement, and up another driveway.

Mo shook himself out as he got out of the passenger seat of the squad car for the seventh time. The boss had given him and Patty a lift up here, which meant he had no transport. Not that he needed it; Uniform were getting used to ferrying him around.

At least he had his own car now, and wasn't reliant on the boss to drive him everywhere like he had been last time they'd been up at Loch Lomond on a murder case. That one had been on the opposite bank. Phineas Montague, internet billionaire, shot while out for a run.

The sergeant he was with turned to look at him as she approached the low house that was their latest stop.

"Everything alright?" she asked him. "You look pale."

"Do I?" He'd felt a touch of motion sickness on the way up; PS Colleen Glover drove fast, taking the bends like she was in a race. "Don't worry, I'm fine."

She shrugged and rang the doorbell. An elderly man opened the door almost immediately.

"I saw you park outside," he said. "Is it about those cars racing along the main road this morning?"

"What cars are those?" PS Glover asked.

The man frowned at her, then at Mo, giving Mo a look that was slightly longer than felt comfortable. "Two cars, haring along there like there was no tomorrow. Wee shites do it early in the morning, when they think there's no one around. One of these days they'll hit someone."

Mo looked back towards the road. He'd heard rumours that Jade's husband had died in a car accident along here, but she never talked about it. Was it one of those 'wee shites' that had hit him?

"Did you happen to see what kind of cars they were?" he asked the man.

"Aye." The man turned back into his house, beckoning for them to follow. "Come on in, and I'll give you the registration numbers."

Mo exchanged glances with Colleen. He followed the man into his house.

The man handed over a scrap of paper with two registration numbers, along with descriptions of the cars. A silver Auris and a red Corsa.

Small cars, to be racing. Maybe they'd been souped up.

"Have you seen them along here before?" Mo asked. "Mr...?"

"Mr Forsythe. Bob Forsythe. And yes, I saw them last

weekend. Same time, same spot. I called it in, but no one came. Why the sudden change?"

"Actually, Mr Forsythe, we're not here about the cars, although they may be relevant to what we're looking into." He tucked the scrap of paper into his jacket pocket. "A body was found on the jetty at Duck Bay this morning, and we're asking if people saw anything suspicious nearby."

"Apart from those cars, nothing. What kind of suspicious?"

"People hanging around who you haven't seen before. Signs of a struggle. Anything that made you concerned."

Mr Forsythe wrinkled his nose and scratched his chin. He had a couple of days' worth of stubble. "Sorry, can't think of anything. Apart from those boy racers. You're going to track them down, aren't you? Throw the book at them?"

"We'll follow it up," Mo told him. Truth was, with a murder investigation on, dangerous driving would be ignored. And without camera evidence...

"You're sure there's nothing else you've seen?" PS Glover asked.

"No, lassie. You got a number I can use, if I think of anything?"

"Sure." She handed over a card.

Outside the house again, Mo looked at the PS. "That number you gave him, what was it?"

"Major Incidents, Loch Lomond and the Trossachs."

"You get a lot of major incidents in the National Park?"

"It's just a phone number. I'm assuming there isn't an incident line for this investigation yet."

"Not that I know of." Mo would tell Jade about the phone number. If calls were going into local CID, they needed to know about it.

His phone rang: the DI.

"Boss," he said. "I'm with Sergeant Glover on door-to-door."

"I don't suppose you've found anyone who's gone missing?"

"Sorry."

"Any unusual activity?" Jade asked.

"Apart from some speeding along the A82, no."

A grunt. "I've been dealing with your old DCI. Something gives me the feeling she's itching to get involved."

"She's on her honeymoon."

"Her honeymoon? So why isn't she shacked up with her husband instead of standing about at a crime scene?"

"Wife," Mo said. "She's married to a woman."

"Oh. Sorry, yes. She did mention that, actually. She gave me her address: the cabins up from the big hotel. Nice spot."

Mo nodded. He wasn't sure how much he wanted to know about the DCI's honeymoon.

"Did she give you any useful information?"

"She did, actually. Registration of a car she spotted near the scene. She was paying attention."

Mo smiled. That was the DCI alright, or what he remembered of her. "You want me to follow it up, find out if the car's registered to an address along here?"

"It's OK. I've passed the details to Patty. You carry on with your door-to-door."

"Will do, boss."

"And let me know if you get a sniff of anything."

"Of course."

CHAPTER SIX

Elsa stepped out of the shower, wrapped herself in her dressing gown and wandered into the bedroom. The cabin had a single mezzanine bedroom with an enormous bed and a small ensuite off. But the best feature was the doors leading out to the balcony over the loch.

She slid over to the railing overlooking the ground floor room.

"Lesley, can you put the coffee machine on?"

No answer.

"Lesley?"

Nothing.

She hurried back to the bed and grabbed the jeans she'd thrown off the night before after they'd arrived in the dark. There was a t-shirt and warm jumper in her bag still; she hadn't unpacked.

Moments later, telling herself not to get annoyed, she arrived at the bottom of the stairs.

When she'd gone into the bathroom, Lesley had been downstairs making breakfast. There was a chance she'd gone to sit outside with it. OK, it was freezing, but there was a view.

Elsa went to the wide windows and peered out, angling herself to get a view of the terrace to the side of the cabin.

The chairs were empty.

She looked around. The ground floor was just one room. Nowhere to hide.

Her hackles rising, she strode to the front door just as there was a knock on it.

Elsa stopped in her tracks.

She scanned the table by the door. Had Lesley gone out and left her keys?

She pulled in a breath and pulled the door open, willing herself to keep her movements measured.

A short Asian man in a suit and blue puffa jacket stood outside. Behind him was a woman in a police uniform.

Elsa frowned. "What's happened? Is Lesley OK?"

The man frowned. "Lesley?"

"My part— my wife. She went out."

"Lesley Clarke?"

"Yes. Are you involved with the body that she found?"

The man held up an ID badge. "Are you Elsa Short?"

Elsa felt a jolt run down her chest. "Yes. Why?"

He shook his head. "I know your name, that's all. You're DCI Clarke's wife."

"Yes, I'm DCI Clarke's wife. Do you know where she is?"

He glanced back at the PC. Elsa looked past him, hoping to see Lesley behind the pair of them.

"Is she with you?" she asked, realising she hadn't listened when Lesley had told her where she'd seen the body. "Did you bring her back?"

"I'm sorry, I haven't seen her. My name's DS Uddin. I

used to work with your wife. Well, for her. Anyway, we're doing house to house, asking people if they've seen anything unusual."

She eyed him. "My wife found a dead body. That's pretty unusual. And now she's disappeared."

"I'm sure she'll be back soon."

"You'd hope so." Elsa looked past him again. There was no point; the fence separating the cabins from the road was behind him. It was locked.

"Sorry," she said. "How did you get past the gate?"

"Oh." He looked back. "The estate office let us through."

"Of course."

"So..." he continued. "Can I ask if you've seen any unusual activity? Boats out on the water showing signs of distress or any kind of struggle? Any sign of a disturbance?"

"I'm sorry, Sergeant. We got here after ten last night. Drove up from Bournemouth. I slept like the dead." She caught herself. "Sorry. You'll tell her to get back here won't you, when you see her?"

"I will." He looked uneasy. Elsa wondered how Lesley would react to being given orders by a DS.

But then, she wasn't on duty today. She was a civilian, on her honeymoon.

And she needed to focus on that, instead of on this damn murder case.

CHAPTER SEVEN

JADE WATCHED as the CSIs and pathologist bent over the body in the water. She was resisting the urge to get closer; she knew how important it was to preserve the scene, and she'd have her chance once they were done.

That woman had watched for a while, after speaking to her. DCI Clarke, from Birmingham, or Dorset, depending on how you looked at it. How many people tried to get involved in murder enquiries while they were on their honeymoon?

Probably a fair few coppers, given half the chance.

A shiver ran through her, remembering her own honeymoon. Mallorca, in August. Seven years ago.

Stop torturing yourself.

Eighteen months had passed since Dan's death. People told her it got easier. People lied.

She wondered if DCI Clarke had been married before. She looked too old for this to be her first marriage.

Maybe Jade was jumping to conclusions. She couldn't imagine a second marriage. Letting someone else into Rory's life like that. He barely remembered his daddy now, the memory resurfacing in occasional mentions of walks by the loch, TV shows they'd watched together. And the birds, of course. Dan had been keen to teach Rory all about birds from before his son could talk.

Focus.

She rubbed her eyes and peered towards the water. Her new unit was based in Glasgow, but was supposed to cover the whole of Scotland. So why did she keep finding herself up here, almost within sight of where it had happened? Another murder case last year had been on the opposite shores of the loch, up past Rowardennan. And now they were here, within ten miles of—

"Jade!" Jamie Douglas, the Crime Scene Manager, was standing up, beckoning her over. Jade hurried towards the water, careful where she trod but relieved to have something to do.

She'd been thinking too much about DCI Clarke. Wondering if she was here on a pretext, but actually angling for Jade's job. It made no sense that the CCU was headed up by a DI.

"Jamie." She stopped a short distance away from the CSM, panting.

"Jade. Good news, if you can call it that."

"An ID?"

"There's a letter in her pocket. It's water damaged, but I reckon it'll be legible after it's been dried out."

"Tell me it's got her name and address on."

"Name and address – and the name of the sender."

"That's enough." Thank God for old-fashioned people, and their hand-written letters. "Hang on. What kind of letter is it?"

Let it be something personal and revealing. Not a council tax payment reminder.

"It's handwritten. The ink has bled significantly, but there's enough. I don't want to open it up again, not till it's somewhere I can get photos."

"OK." Jade looked back towards the road. "There must be somewhere we can use."

Jamie nodded in the same direction. "We're setting up a tent. A bigger one."

Jade looked towards the pathologist, Dr Pradesh. "I take it you're not doubting it was murder."

Dr Pradesh looked up, causing the water to move and the body to shift. "Not a doubt. I wanted to be sure it wasn't an accident. It might have been done by the rudder of a boat. But no. You see that shape there, on the side of her head?"

There was a bruise on the side of the victim's head, not far from the mess that had once been her face. It was almost circular.

"A hammer," Jade said.

"I reckon. We'll know more after the post-mortem."

Jade surveyed the victim's head, the colour of her skin. "She'd have lost a lot of blood."

"And sustained significant brain damage. I imagine that's what killed her. Horrible." The pathologist crossed himself. Jade hadn't pegged him as a Catholic. She needed to resist coming to assumptions about people.

She sniffed. "Thanks. Let's get started on this letter, then."

CHAPTER EIGHT

Mo SHUT the gate leading to the cabin the DCI was staying in, and trudged up the road towards the squad car. Sergeant Glover was knocking on doors further along, asking if anyone had seen anything unusual. He stopped at the car, peering along the driveway leading to another set of holiday homes.

All holiday homes. Did anyone other than Jade actually live around here?

"DS Uddin!"

He turned to see DCI Clarke heading towards him, from the direction of the crime scene. He stiffened. The DCI was still a senior member of Force CID to him. Zoe's boss. Treating her as a member of the public didn't sit easy with him.

"Ma'am," he said as she approached.

She shook her head. "I'm on holiday, Mo. And I'm a member of the public." She hesitated. "Do I even have rank, here in Scotland?"

"You do, Ma'am. I only had to do some conversion training when I moved up."

"Of course. What made you move? The fallout from the whole Randle business?"

He cleared his throat. Zoe hadn't told him how closely the DCI had been involved in all that. Randle had been DCI Clarke's senior officer.

"Family," he said. "My parents-in-law aren't well. My wife got a transfer to Stirling."

A smile. He didn't remember the DCI smiling much when she'd been in Birmingham. "Well, I hope Scotland is treating you well. I gave a statement to your new boss, DI Tanner. You need me to add more detail?"

"I was doing door-to-door. Spoke to your wife."

The smile widened. "Elsa. I don't suppose she had anything to tell you."

"No."

"No." She cocked her head. "Are you confident DI Tanner can solve this? It's a nasty one."

He stiffened. "I am."

"She as good as Zoe? Can't be as much fun to work with, given that you and Zoe were mates."

Still are. He eyed her. "It's not a competition."

"You're right, it's not. Well, let me know if you do need anything else from me." She walked past him and towards the gate. Mo turned to see PS Glover walking down the slope towards them. He felt his muscles relax.

"Thanks, Ma'am," he said.

"Lesley." She gave him a pointed look, then disappeared through the gate.

"Who was that?" Colleen asked. "She see anything?"

"That was the woman who found the body."

A whistle. "A holidaymaker?"

"My old boss. From Birmingham."

The sergeant's eyes widened. "Small world."

Mo said nothing. He opened the door to the car as his phone rang: Jade. Thank God.

"Boss."

"You with Uniform?"

"I am."

"I could tell."

"Anything to report?" he asked, ignoring Colleen's gaze on him.

"We've got an ID. Her name was Helen Williamson. Twenty-three years old, local."

Mo winced. Twenty-three. He clenched a fist and mouthed 'ID' at the sergeant. She nodded in acknowledgement.

"You need me to do anything?" he asked.

"Go see the family. They're not far away."

Mo felt his shoulders sag. "There isn't an FLO?"

"Take Sergeant Glover."

"Will do."

"And Mo?"

Colleen had started the car. Mo buckled in, his phone to his ear. "Yes?"

"Your old DCI, is she going to give us any trouble?"

"What kind of trouble?"

"I need to know she's not going to try and run a parallel investigation."

Mo looked in the wing mirror as they drove towards the A82. He could see the locked gate.

"She's on her honeymoon. I don't think there'll be a problem."

"Good."

CHAPTER NINE

JADE SAT IN HER CAR, gazing at the sky over the loch. It was a grey day, much like any other on Loch Lomond. Given that it was March, she was lucky it wasn't raining.

She should check the weather overnight. It might have made a difference to the state of the victim's – Helen's – body.

She narrowed her eyes. *Twenty-three*. And how were they going to show the body to the family, in the state her face was in?

She dialled Petra.

"Jade. Don't tell me, you've got work for me."

"A murder at Loch Lomond."

"Another one?"

"We've got an ID on the body."

"That's good. But that's not what you're calling me for."

Jade smiled to herself. She liked that Petra didn't wait to be asked.

"No," she said. "I've got a letter. We're getting the forensics folk to work on it, see if they can decipher it. But I'd like your take on the psychology."

"A suicide note?"

"A *Dear John* letter."

"Oh." Petra's voice had brightened. "Is it dated?"

"Three days ago."

"And who's it from? I assume it's addressed to the victim, not a letter she wrote and didn't send."

"It's to her. Her name was Helen, she was twenty-three."

"I do love old-fashioned communications," Petra said. "Male or female?"

"Sorry?"

"The sender. Male or female?"

"Male. Name of Rob. We still need to work out exactly who he is, but it shouldn't be hard. Assuming he lives locally."

"He might not."

Petra had a point. The psychologist herself had girl-friends all over the world, it seemed. Or at least she had done, in the past.

"I think there might be issues in the family, too," Jade said. "The letter alludes to the relationship being a secret from the victim's brother."

"Ah. Send it over to me, and I'll let you know what I think."

"That's the thing." Jade bit her bottom lip. "When did you say you were heading to France?"

"Not for a few days. You need me to talk to the family for you?"

"I need you to sit in while DS Uddin talks to them."

"OK. I'll take a train to Balloch."

"We can send a squad car for you."

"Nice."

Jade could hear the smile in Petra's voice.

"I'll be there in forty-five minutes or so," Petra said. "Assuming your squad car can break a speed limit once or twice."

CHAPTER TEN

"This is nice." Elsa slid her arm into Lesley's and cuddled up to her wife as they walked.

Lesley looked at Elsa and smiled. "It is." She stopped walking for a brief kiss.

"Did they get a statement from you?" Elsa asked as they continued walking along the loch. "I hope they're finished with you."

"They did." Lesley picked up pace. "Did DS Uddin talk to you?"

"He was doing door-to-door. Routine stuff. I didn't know anything." Elsa gave her a sidelong glance. "I'd only just stepped out of the shower."

"They've got an ID. On the victim."

"That's good for them." Elsa's voice was tight. "I suppose."

"A young woman, lives locally."

Elsa stopped to face Lesley. "How do you know all this?"

Lesley felt her face heat up. "I overheard Mo on the phone."

Elsa raised an eyebrow. "Really?"

"Really." Lesley turned to look ahead. They'd driven to Balloch, then decided to go for a walk. There was a tourist shopping mall on the banks of the loch, and Lesley had wanted to pick up a gift for Sharon. She'd bought her a plush highland cow. A little too young for her, perhaps, but probably not.

"Stop." Elsa tugged on Lesley's arm.

Lesley did so, almost stumbling. "What?"

Elsa was looking ahead, along the loch. "That's the crime scene."

Lesley followed Elsa's gaze. A forensics tent had been erected over the jetty where she'd found the body. Two squad cars and a CSI van were on the sliproad leading to the main road.

"You brought me here deliberately," Elsa said.

"I didn't, love. I wanted to buy that present for Sharon. It was your idea to—"

"You encouraged it." Elsa pulled her arm loose from Lesley's grip. "We could have walked the other way. Around the loch."

"The woods. We both thought they—"

"And then when we'd walked through the woods, we carried on going. You should have told me to stop."

"Elsa sweetie, it's just a walk. I thought that was part of the point of coming here?"

"There are plenty of walks around here, and you know it. You deliberately brought me along this way so you could see what was happening."

"I..."

Lesley stopped herself.

Even if she hadn't deliberately walked Elsa up here, she knew that her subconscious wanted to check on progress.

She was a copper. She couldn't help herself.

"I'm sorry. Let's go back."

"Let's."

Elsa turned to walk back towards Balloch, her pace brisk. Lesley hurried to keep up.

"Let's walk round the other way," she suggested. "We can go back to the shops, then carry on round the water's edge."

"I want to go back to the car."

"Els, please—"

"Don't. Let's not talk till we get back. Maybe that way we can enjoy the rest of our trip."

CHAPTER ELEVEN

Mo hated doing this.

He gave Sergeant Glover a grim smile as the two of them stood on the doorstep of Helen Williamson's family home. He could feel a lump forming in his throat, his knees loosening.

The door opened and a friendly-looking woman in her fifties smiled out at them. Mo swallowed the lump in his throat.

"Hello. How can I help you?" Her expression dropped as she took in Colleen's uniform. "Oh. It'll be about the body you found down by the loch. Nasty business." She sucked her teeth.

Mo held up his ID. "Mrs Williamson?"

She nodded. "Gail."

"My name's Detective Sergeant Uddin. This is Sergeant Glover."

"You don't sound like you come from round these parts."

"I'm from Birmingham."

"Ah. Well, all welcome here. How can I help you?"

"Can we come in in, please?" Colleen asked. She was peering around the woman, trying to see if anyone else was inside.

"Of course. Hang on a wee while, I'll make you a cup of tea."

"It's fine," Mo said. "We just want to talk."

"You'll be in a hurry. Of course." The woman held the door open for them, then ushered them towards a door to one side. The hallway was narrow and dark, with family photos on the walls. Mo made out one of a young woman. Helen? He had no idea, as her facial injuries had rendered her unrecognisable.

He closed his eyes. *Poor woman.*

A young man came down the stairs, his footsteps heavy. "What's going on? Ma, who are these?"

"It's alright, son. It's just the police. They're doing door-to-door."

"Hmm." He gave Mo a look, then headed through another door into a kitchen.

In the living room, the woman stood looking between them, her hands clasped in front of her. "So you'll be wanting to know if I've seen anything odd."

Mo gave her a tight smile. "Let's take a seat."

Her face darkened. "Why?"

"Please."

PS Glover sat on the chair closest to Mrs Williamson and Mo took a perch at the end of the sofa. Mrs Williamson sat along from him. She was squeezing her hands together.

"What is it? Tell me."

"I'm very sorry, Mrs Williamson, bu—"

The woman let out a wail. She held up her hand. "Stop. I don't want to hear it."

The door opened: the young man. A brother, perhaps. "What's up, Ma?"

His mother beckoned him to her, her eyes squeezed shut. "Talk to them, Callum. I can't."

He stood next to his mum, a hand on her shoulder. Supportive, or possessive? "What d'ye want?"

"My name's DS Uddin and this is PS Glover. Can I ask your name?"

"Callum." He looked at his mum, then back to Mo. "What is this?"

"I'm very sorry to tell you this, Callum, but your sister's been found dead."

Another wail from Gail, twice as loud as the first.

"It's OK, Ma." Callum rubbed her shoulder. "They're wrong." He glared at Mo. "She's still in bed. She went out clubbing last night and she always sleeps in."

"It's past lunchtime." Gail's voice was flat.

"She's done it before." He left his mother's side and stormed out of the room. Mo and Colleen sat in silence as the woman wept on the sofa.

Heavy footsteps receded up the stairs, paused, then approached again. Mo clenched a fist in his lap.

"Sergeant Glover here will be able to support you," he said, leaning over towards the woman. "She's an exce—"

The door flew open. "You bastards."

Mo stood up. "I'm so sorry."

The young man was shaking his head, his lips tight and his face pale. "You bastards." He looked at his mum. "She's no' there, Ma. She's feckin' gone."

CHAPTER TWELVE

"THANKS, PAL." Petra climbed out of the squad car. The young constable who'd driven her up had certainly known how to drive fast. And Petra didn't have so much as a hair out of place.

She paused outside the car, peering back into the passenger window to check her reflection. Her updo was intact, secured by half a can of hairspray as usual. She dabbed at her lipstick and rubbed her lips together.

You'll do.

And besides, this family had just lost their daughter. They wouldn't give two figs what she looked like.

She walked up the footpath, her heels catching in the gravel, and rang the doorbell. A uniformed sergeant answered the door.

"I'm Dr McBride," she said. "DI Tanner asked me to—"

"It's fine," the woman replied. "DS Uddin said to expect you. Come in."

The sergeant led Petra through to a dining room at the back of the house. Mo sat at the table, a laptop open in front of him. So they'd set up shop here, in the victim's home. The family wouldn't have been happy about that.

Did it mean they suspected a family member, were expecting a quick arrest?

She wasn't about to ask. Knowing what the police were thinking would jeopardise her impartiality.

She put a hand out as Mo stood up from his chair.

"DS Uddin," she said. "Good to see you again."

"If only it could be in more pleasant circumstances."

"True. But it never will be, will it?" Petra took a chair opposite him and brought out a notepad. "I don't want to trouble these people any longer than I have to. Tell me what you know about them. But don't give me your theories. Not yet."

Mo closed his mouth, glanced at the sergeant, then nodded. "OK," he said, his voice low. "Our victim is Helen Williamson." He pushed a photograph across the table. "Her body was found under a jetty on Loch Lomond early this morning, by a DCI from the Dorset force who's here on holiday."

"Lesley." Petra raised an eyebrow. "Quite a coincidence."

"Sorry, I forgot you two know each other."

"I worked on a couple of her Dorset cases. Not just your Digbeth Ripper one."

"It wasn't the Dig—"

She waved a hand. "That doesn't matter now. Keep going."

"Helen's face was cut up, so badly she's unrecognisable. But we found a letter in her pocket, handwritten, from someone called Rob. The mother tells us that's probably Rob Cowie, her boyfriend."

"OK. He here?"

"No."

"He around? Can I see the letter?"

"You can." Mo passed another sheet of paper across the table, a copy of a handwritten note. Petra peered at it then back at him.

"Have the family seen this?"

"We didn't think that would be a good idea until we'd spoken to the boyfriend."

"Ex-boyfriend. Judging by this letter."

Mo tightened his lips. "Yes."

"OK," Petra said. "So he sent her a letter dumping her, which she had in her pocket. That either means it's recent, or she wanted to keep the letter close for some reason. I don't suppose you've...?"

"We were waiting for you to get here."

"OK. Well I can't ask questions, you know that. But I can advise, and I can sit in."

"We need to talk to the mother and the brother," Mo told her.

"Have you kept them apart?"

"That seemed heartless," the uniformed sergeant said.

Petra sighed, looking at the woman. "What's your name?"

The woman straightened. "PS Glover, Ma'am."

"I'm not your senior officer, you can call me Dr McBride."

"Doctor."

"The fact that you've let them be together means they can confer. Do you know what percentage of murders are committed by a family member, Sergeant?"

PS Glover gave Mo a sidelong glance. "Most of them."

"I was hoping for something more specific," Petra said,

"but yes, *most* of them. Which means the mother or the brother might well have done it." She shook her head. "Right. So I suggest you find out what you can about the relationship with the boyfriend, and what the family thought of it. Ask that before mentioning the letter. They might not know he dumped her. If they volunteer that information, it'll be useful. It might give them a motive."

"A mother doesn't kill her daughter because a boyfriend has dumped her," Mo said.

"No. But there might have been some kind of confrontation which went wrong. You can't rule anything out."

"The state of her face," the sergeant said. "That's not accidental."

Petra looked down at the photo. She felt a muscle in her cheek twitch. The sergeant had a point.

"I'll go slowly," Mo said, "build up to the letter and the relationship status. If you think I'm headed in the wrong direction, cough."

Petra snorted. "Subtle."

"Is there another signal you'd like to use?"

"Coughing's fine. Let's get to it."

CHAPTER THIRTEEN

THE POST-MORTEM WAS BEING CARRIED out at Queen Elizabeth Hospital in Glasgow, meaning a forty-five minute drive for Jade. It felt good to get back onto busy roads and away from the constant presence of the loch. She decided not to think too deeply about what that might mean for her decision to carry on living there.

She'd get used to it.

She stood at the back of the room, watching Dr Pradesh go through the motions of examining the body, removing and analysing organs and looking at toxicology. In the end, cause of death was pronounced to be exactly what they all knew it would be: blood loss following the injuries to the face and head.

She headed out of the building, gulping in the fresh air. No copper liked post-mortems, and Jade had found this one more uncomfortable than most. Since starting at the CCU, she'd delegated attendance at them to her team, preferring not to be reminded of the time she'd had to come to one of these places and identify her own husband.

She rubbed her arms. The sun had come out and she wore a heavy waterproof coat, but she was chilly nonetheless. She would head back to the office, confer with Patty and Stuart. It meant almost an hour more driving, but she didn't want to leave them alone without any momentum.

As she got into her car, the phone rang: an unfamiliar number.

"DI Tanner." She started the ignition and hit hands-free.

"DI Tanner, it's Lesley Clarke."

Jade thought for a moment, then remembered. "DCI Clarke. How are you? Is there some new information you need to provide?"

"Sorry, no. I just wanted to get an update on how things were going. Have you found the poor girl's killer yet?"

"I'm afraid not. We're making progress on the investigation, though. I'm afraid I can't discuss details."

"You're talking to her family. Do you suspect one of them?"

Jade turned onto the M8, drumming her fingers on the steering wheel. Did DCI Clarke know that Mo and Petra were at the Williamson house, or was she drawing conclusions based on her own knowledge of how these things were done?

Don't be so paranoid.

"I'm sure you understand I can't discuss whether we have a suspect."

"Well, if I can be of any help..."

"If you have more information about the circumstances in which you found the body, or anything you might have seen this morning, then I'd be very grateful for it. Do you want me to send an officer to your cabin?"

"No no, it's fine. I told you everything I know."

Why am I not surprised?

DCI Clarke was just trying to stick her oar in.

And Jade wasn't about to let her.

"I'm grateful for your help, Ma'am. If I have anything else I need your input on, I'll call you."

She hung up.

Had she been rude?

DCI Clarke was a senior officer, after all. And she'd been Mo's boss.

Jade shook her head as the motorway crossed the Clyde. DCI Clarke wasn't her concern, and she wasn't Mo's any longer.

CHAPTER FOURTEEN

GAIL AND CALLUM WILLIAMSON sat beside one another on the sofa in their living room. They'd been joined by Gail's husband Jim, who squeezed in next to his wife. The room was sparse, furnished only by the three-piece suite, a side table, a low TV unit, and a crucifix on the wall.

Mo and Petra each sat in an armchair, both of which had been pulled round so that they almost faced the sofa. The room was quiet. No TV, no radio from another room, no sounds from upstairs.

"We're so sorry for your loss," Mo said, looking at Jim Williamson. The man had arrived home from his work at a warehouse in Dumbarton half an hour earlier.

Jim grunted.

"I don't understand," Gail said. "We've already told you about Rob. He dumped her. Surely it's him you should be talking to, not us."

"And we will do, Mrs Williamson. Don't worry."

A squad car had been sent to Rob Cowie's house in

Alexandria, and Stuart wasn't far behind it. Hopefully, as another young man, he'd be able to get Rob to open up.

"You tell that wee shite—" Jim began, but was stopped by his wife putting a hand on his knee.

"Jim. Let the officer speak." She sniffed.

Mo gave her a sympathetic smile. Colleen was in the kitchen, tidying up and keeping herself busy. She'd been assigned as the Family Liaison Officer and he knew she'd be his eyes and ears in the house after he and Petra left.

"We just want to find out what Helen's movements were yesterday. She works at the Loch Lomond Shores shopping mall in Balloch, is that right?"

Gail nodded. "She got a job in Sports Direct six months ago. She's got Highers, I always thought she could do better, but she seems happy enough." Her voice wavered. "Seemed."

Mo wrote down the name of the shop on his pad. They would need to speak to the manager, and to Helen's colleagues.

"What time did her shift finish?"

"Six thirty. She normally came straight home, although sometimes Rob picked her up and took her out."

"Where did they usually go?"

A shake of the head. "She was twenty-three, detective. She didn't tell us that kind of thing."

"Glasgow," Callum muttered. "They went to Glasgow."

"No, pet. They can't have gone all that way just for a night out."

"They did." He looked Mo in the face. "Sauchiehall Street. Merchant City sometimes. They went out clubbing." He glanced at his mum. "Didn't get in till the early hours. That's why I thought she was still asleep."

Mo smiled at him. "Thanks. Are there any particular clubs they often went to?"

Callum's eyes narrowed. "She mentioned a few." He gave the names of some clubs. "And they went to a new one last week, the Nightbird."

Mo wrote down the names on his pad. More interviews. Would they have to put out an appeal for eye witnesses, in Glasgow? That would be like looking for a needle in a haystack. They still needed to determine where Helen had been when she died.

"Did she say where they were planning on going last night?"

Callum shook his head and scratched his chin. "I hadn't spoken to her for a few days. We—"

His mum put a hand on his arm. "Don't trouble yourself about that, son."

He nodded and looked down.

"Sorry," said Mo. "What were you about to tell me?" He could sense Petra straightening in her chair, listening carefully and taking copious notes. The family's eyes kept flicking to her, no doubt wondering who she was. A colleague, was all he'd said.

"We fell out." Callum looked at Mo. "I didn't like Rob. He treated her wrong. He's the one you should be talking to. Not us."

"Why's that?"

"He was violent. Slapped her a couple of times."

Mo had spoken to Jade before this interview, and looked at the preliminary report from the pathologist. Other than the wounds that had killed her, there had been no sign of bruising on Helen's body. No evidence of abuse.

"How often did he slap her?" he asked.

A shrug. "Couple of times, in the last month. He was careful, though. Didn't do it where people would see."

Mo nodded. "She told you about it?"

"She did." Callum leaned back, his gaze still on Mo. It was like a challenge. What was he hiding?

"And he got her pregnant," Jim said, making Gail gasp.

"Jim," she muttered, "we weren't going to—"

"They'll know about it," he said. "You're doing a post-mortem, aren't you?"

"Yes," Mo replied.

Jade had emailed him the report. If Helen Williamson had been pregnant, he'd have known about it.

"So when did she tell you she was pregnant?"

Jim shook his head. "She didn't. But I saw the test under her bed."

"You often look under your sister's bed?"

He gave her a look.

"I told him to fetch her washing down," Gail said. "A week ago. He brought the washing, and the stick."

Mo exchanged glances with Petra. She was chewing her lip, her hair coming loose on top of her head.

"Did you ask her about it?" he asked.

Gail looked down. "No. I was waiting for the right time." She looked up, her eyes red. "Hoping she'd confide in me."

"The shite," Callum muttered. "Doing that to my sister."

"How did you react?" Mo asked, looking at the young man.

"I wanted to look after my little sister," he replied. "Wouldn't you?"

Mo had come across this kind of protectiveness before, in family members. It could spill over into revenge.

But if Callum had wanted revenge, then surely he'd have wanted it on Rob, not on his sister?

"I tell you," Gail said. "I resisted talking ill of him to Helen, but he was bad for her. It's him you want to be talking to."

CHAPTER FIFTEEN

Stuart walked back to his car from Rob Cowie's house, pulling his jacket tighter around his shoulders.

At the car, he stopped and looked back up at the house. The bedroom curtains were open, no light or sign of movement.

He'd knocked once, peered in through the obscured glazing, knocked again then lifted the letterbox.

There was no one in.

So why was there a car on the drive?

He got into his car and checked his notes. There had been cars seen around the time of the murder, but he couldn't remember what.

Two cars racing up the A82, spotted by a local fella. A silver Auris and a red Corsa.

He eyed the car sitting on the driveway. It was neither of those models.

He flicked further through his notes. DCI Clarke had seen a car pull away from the loch, just after spotting the body...

A silver Aygo, she'd said.

He looked at the car.

It was a silver Aygo.

He shoved open his door and strode to the car. He looked into it, careful not to make contact.

The car was clean. A few scraps of litter in the footwell, an old coffee cup between the seats.

But no blood. No sign someone had been killed and then transported in it.

He walked round to the boot.

They'd need a warrant to open it. Or the permission of the owner.

They'd also need forensics techs. Not him.

He went back to his car, grateful for the heating, and dialled the DI.

"Stuart," she said. "You spoken to the boyfriend yet?"

"No," he said. "But I've got something else for you."

CHAPTER SIXTEEN

It got dark early in Scotland. Lesley and Elsa hadn't even started to discuss where they were going to have dinner when dusk descended upon the loch like a blanket.

Lesley gazed out of the windows of the cabin, peering over at dim lights on the opposite shore. Birds skimmed across the surface of the water, their wingbeats silent beyond the thick glass.

"Let's go out for dinner," she said. "There's a pub in Luss I read about, it loo—"

"I'm too tired." Elsa sat on the sofa, reading a book and barely making eye contact.

"Els," Lesley said," I've apologised a hundred times. I told you I'd leave it alone. Please, talk to me."

Elsa looked over her book. "I *am* talking to you. I'm telling you I don't want to go out for dinner." She gazed at Lesley for a moment, then lowered her book. "Let's stay in. Have a quiet night."

"Reading, or eating together?"

Elsa considered a moment. "Eating together." She put the book down. "I'm sorry. I'm being grumpy. It's just you promised me there would be no murder cases on our honeymoon."

"And I wasn't expecting there to be any." Lesley went to the sofa and sat down. She put a hand on Elsa's knee. Elsa placed her own hand on top of it, making Lesley sigh with relief. She'd been worrying that they'd have their first marital spat within days of the wedding.

She turned her palm upwards and squeezed Elsa's hand. Elsa squeezed back.

"We OK?" Lesley asked.

"We are." Elsa leaned over and gave her a kiss. "I still want to stay in, though. Why don't you go out, see if you can get us a takeaway."

"OK. We can go to the pub tomorrow."

"Lunch." Elsa smiled at her.

"Lunch." Lesley kissed her wife then went to grab her coat.

Ten minutes later she was in the car park on the edge of Luss, checking Google Maps and trying to work out what takeaway might be available. Luss wasn't exactly Birmingham, or even Bournemouth. She'd checked JustEat and found nothing.

She walked into the village, taking in the scent of wood burning and the sight of smoke rising from a couple of chimneys. This *definitely* wasn't Birmingham.

She turned a corner and stopped. A squad car was parked in the road just ahead of her.

A routine stop, or something to do with the murder case?

She should ignore it.

Pretend she'd never seen it, turn the other way, and continue with her evening.

Bollocks to that.

She carried on walking towards the car, slowing her pace as she approached.

The car was outside a house whose front windows were lit from within, the curtains closed.

Lesley stopped as the front door opened. She hung back as a man emerged.

The man was tall and heavily built, wearing a dark coat with the hood pulled up. He hunched his shoulders, not looking around as he walked away from the house. He carried a bin bag.

Lesley pulled into the shadow of another house, waiting for the man to put the bin bag into the wheelie bin at the side of his house. But he didn't. Instead he walked right past it and along the street, away from her.

The bin bag was almost empty but seemed to contain something heavy. It swung at his side, occasionally hitting his leg and making him grimace.

She walked a few metres behind the man. He took two left turns, eventually ending up back at the car park on the outskirts of the village.

Lesley stood by a set of public toilets, making sure she didn't step into the pool of light in front of them. She watched the man walk to a litter bin, look around, and then place the bin bag inside it.

She held her breath as he turned back towards her. Quickly, she scuttled around the back of the public toilet, narrowly avoiding being seen. He walked back in the direction he'd come.

She emerged from behind the toilet building and stared

at the litter bin. The man had been empty-handed when he'd passed her. Whatever he'd been carrying in that bin bag was in the litter bin. And for some reason, he hadn't wanted to put it in his own bin at home.

She looked towards the bin, then back where the man had gone. Should she follow him, check he went back to the house? Knock on the door and identify him?

Or should she go to the bin, find out what he'd dumped there?

She pulled out her phone and dialled the number on the card Jade Tanner had given her as she ran towards the bin. The car park was quiet, only two cars apart from her own and no sign of people.

The phone rang out.

Pick up, pick up.

She reached the bin just as the phone was answered.

"DI Tanner."

"DI Tanner, it's Lesley Clarke."

"DCI Clarke. How can I help you?"

Lesley could hear the exasperation in the woman's voice.

"Where are you?" Lesley asked, thinking of the squad car she'd seen.

She opened the litter bin. The bin bag was at the top.

"I'm at our office," DI Tanner replied. "I don't see how that's relevant."

Lesley frowned. She needed to cover her hands.

She reached into her pocket and brought out a plastic bag. She wedged the phone between her ear and shoulder.

"DI Tanner, I may have some crucial evidence for you."

"Which you didn't see fit to tell me about earlier."

"It's new."

With her hand tightly wrapped in the plastic bag, Lesley carefully opened the bin bag. She almost dropped her phone.

"DI Tanner, I think I've found your murder weapon."

CHAPTER SEVENTEEN

JADE WAS over an hour from Luss when Lesley had called her. She'd been pulling into the car park on the business park where the Complex Crime Unit's office was, intending to go in and speak to Patty about the case.

She stopped the car across four spaces, her heart pounding in her ears.

A hammer, DCI Clarke had said. A man had emerged from a house in Luss, a house with a squad car outside. Then he'd dumped a hammer in a litter bin.

There was only one house it could be.

She started the ignition and called Patty.

"I'm just outside," she told the DC. "Sorry, but I don't have time to come in. I need to get back up to the crime scene."

"They've found forensics?"

"DCI Clarke has." Jade felt her chest tighten. She'd been irritated at Lesley getting involved. Now the woman uncovered a key piece of evidence. She could only hope that she'd done as Jade had told her and left it alone as soon as she'd ended the call.

Of course she had. She was a serving DCI in a major crime investigation unit. She knew how these things worked.

"I'm heading up to Luss," she said. "Call Mo and Stuart and let them know."

"Why?"

Jade ran through what Lesley had told her: the man emerging from the house, the weapon dumped in a litter bin.

"I'll get Jamie Douglas there too."

"No," said Jade. "Not him, we don't want cross contamination. One of his team. Heather, she wasn't at the first crime scene."

She considered. She and Mo had both been at the crime scene. Mo had been at the Williamson house. And Stuart had gone to see Helen's boyfriend.

But the hammer was covered in blood, DCI Clarke had said. And now they had an eyewitness account, a reliable one, too.

She didn't need to worry.

"I'll call Fraser," she said. "Get a warrant."

"OK. I'll let Jamie know."

"Thanks, Patty. And I'm sorry I wasn't able to come back to the office."

"It's alright. You're not coming back afterwards, I hope."

Jade sighed. She was back on the M8, high over the city centre. How long would it take to drive through the city and out the other side?

"I'll have to."

"Don't be daft, boss."

Jade smiled. She and Patty had worked together for years. They'd been colleagues in Strathclyde CID before the formation of the CCU. Patty mothered her, despite the rank difference.

"I'll be fine, Patty. My mum can have Rory."

Patty said nothing. Jade hoped the DC wasn't judging her. Being single mum to a young son as well as a DI wasn't easy.

"Call Jamie," she said. "Remind him not to come himself, to send Heather instead. I'll get the warrant." She looked at her dashboard clock: just gone 7pm. Barely more than twelve hours since the body had been found.

She'd proven herself. And given a young woman justice.

So why did she not feel better about it?

CHAPTER EIGHTEEN

LESLEY WASN'T GOING ANYWHERE until the police turned up. She sat in her car, huddling against the cold and watching the litter bin.

After calling Jade, she'd closed the bag and lowered the bin lid, careful not to disturb anything else. She'd scanned the ground in case the man she'd seen had left shoe prints.

He'd come out of that house, the one with the squad car outside. She had no idea whose house it was, but it was likely he lived there.

Still, she hoped he'd left fingerprints on that bin bag.

She thought for a moment. Had he been wearing gloves?

Of course he had.

But he might not have been wearing them when he first opened the pack of bags. He might not have been when he bought them. He might not have been when he put the hammer inside.

All of it would add up.

She scanned the buildings around the car park. There was a camera on the toilet block: CCTV.

Perfect.

Her phone rang: Elsa.

Damn. She should have told her.

"Hi, love. Sorry I'm not back yet."

"You OK? I was worried."

"Look." Lesley tightened her grip on the wheel. "I saw something in Luss. A man carrying what might be a murder weapon."

"Yes?" Elsa's voice was hesitant.

"I was trying to find somewhere I could pick up some food. A chippy. But I saw him come out of a house when I was walking through the village."

"You just happened to see him."

"It was a coincidence, sweetie. I promise. I'm watching the litter bin he dumped it in, then I'll get back to you as soon as local police arrive."

"And how long will that take?"

"You're pissed off with me."

"I'm hungry."

And pissed off. "I don't know," Lesley replied.

She thought back to the squad car, outside the house. She could go there, bring the officers back with her.

But she had to make sure no one disturbed that bin bag.

Lights passed as a car entered the car park. It wasn't a squad car. She could only hope it was a detective.

A man got out. He looked at his phone for a moment, then approached her car.

"Elsa love, they're here. I won't be long."

She hung up and got out of the car.

"DCI Clarke?" the man asked. He was young, with ruddy cheeks and hair that looked like no amount of product would smooth it down.

"That's me. You are...?"

"DC Stuart Burns, Ma'am. DI Tanner sent me." He looked around the car park. "Where's this murder weapon?"

CHAPTER NINETEEN

Mo was in the Williamsons' dining room with Petra and Colleen. The victim's parents were in the living room, and her brother had gone to his room. Colleen kept coming in and out, ostensibly delivering cups of tea but really keeping an eye on the family.

"What do you think?" he asked Petra.

"We need to find out what the boyfriend has to say for himself. If he knew about the pregnancy."

"The PM found no sign of a pregnancy."

Petra nodded. She'd know that was one of the first things the pathologist looked for, when a victim was a young woman.

"So what about the test?" Mo asked.

"A miscarriage?" suggested Colleen.

"She was a virgin," Petra said. "I've read the report and there's no sign of her ever having engaged in sexual activity."

Colleen turned to her. "She was twenty-three."

"Not everyone has sex at a young age."

"She had a boyfriend."

"That doesn't mean anything." The psychologist gave the PC a disdainful look. "We aren't all itching to jump in and out of each other's pants."

Mo looked at the doctor. Since he'd met her, she'd had at least three girlfriends. But now she was speaking professionally, not personally.

And besides, it was none of his business.

He frowned, remembering the living room. He looked round the dining room. Sure enough, the only item on the wall in here was religious too: a Madonna.

He grabbed his phone and dialled Stuart.

"Stuart, have you spoken to the boyfriend yet?"

"Sorry, sarge. No sign of anyone in the house. I'm in the car park at Luss, with DCI Clarke. The DI called, told me to get over here."

"How long were you at the house?"

"Ninety minutes."

"He works at the Morrisons in Helensburgh. Have you checked with them?"

"I called them before I came up here. He finished his shift three hours ago."

So where was Rob Cowie? Mo balled his fist on the table.

He heard voices outside and looked up. Colleen exchanged glances with him then slipped out of the room. The voices intensified.

He could hear Colleen's voice, low and cool, trying to smooth the waters. To de-escalate, as a FLO was trained to do.

But to de-escalate what?

"Stay here," he told Petra. He followed Colleen out into the hallway.

Jim Williamson was at the bottom of the stairs. His son

Callum was just inside the front door, wearing a dark coat and gloves. Cold air drifted off him.

He'd gone out, and they hadn't known.

Mo glanced at Colleen. She looked embarrassed.

The family wasn't under house arrest. Of course not. But he preferred to know where family members were, in the immediate aftermath of a murder.

"Where did you go?" Jim was asking his son. "You were supposed to be in your room."

"I needed a walk."

"You don't walk anywhere."

Colleen stepped forward. "I'm sure there's nothing to worry about, Mr Williamson. Callum, if you don't mind telling me where you were, that would be helpful."

He glared at her. "I've told you where I was when my sister died. Surely that's enough."

Mo's phone rang: the DI. He walked away, speaking quietly so as not to be overheard.

"Boss," he said. "I'm at the Williamson House—"

"That's exactly where I need you. Has anyone left the house in the last hour?"

He looked at Callum.

"Yes," he replied. "Helen's brother."

"I thought as much."

"Why?"

"He was seen dumping a blood-stained hammer in a litter bin near the house," the DI told him.

"The murder weapon." Mo blinked, staring at Callum. "What d'you need me to do, boss?"

"I've spoken to Detective Superintendent Murdo and we have a warrant. Mo, arrest him."

CHAPTER TWENTY

LESLEY BREATHED in the cold air on the cabin's deck. A cup of coffee was cooling on the table in front of her.

She folded her arms around herself and turned as the door to the cabin opened.

"Sweetie."

"I heard you get out of bed. I decided to follow you down today, so you can't go finding any more bodies."

"I'm sorry, love."

Elsa put one hand on Lesley's shoulder and drank her coffee with the other. "It's OK. I'd have done the same."

"Would you?"

Elsa sat in the second chair, her hand sliding down Lesley's arm. "Maybe I'd have come at it differently. I'm a defence lawyer, not a detective. But I'm just as drawn to this stuff as you are."

Lesley smiled at her. "So we're well matched."

"We are. Perfectly."

Lesley felt the muscles in her face relax. "I was so

worried that you'd hate me. I made you a promise, and then I broke it. On our honeymoon."

"You promised there'd be no murders in Scotland while we were here. It wasn't exactly your fault that someone else had better ideas."

Lesley put her coffee down. She leaned across and stroked Elsa's cheek. "I love you, sweetie."

"I know. And I love you too."

CHAPTER TWENTY-ONE

JADE SAT in her car outside the Williamson house, watching white-suited techs come and go. Traces of blood had been found in Helen's bedroom, and the whole house was being thoroughly examined.

The passenger door opened and Stuart got in. "Heya, boss."

"Stuart," she said. "How are the interviews going?"

"The sarge and Patty have spoken to Callum. I'll be having another chat with Rob later on, but I've sent you his initial statement."

She nodded. "He says the pregnancy was faked."

"Yeah."

Jade's mind went to her own test, the morning she'd discovered she was expecting Rory. "Why would you do that?"

"She wanted to move in with him," Stuart replied. "Leave the family. They wouldn't let her. But she reckoned that if they thought she was pregnant, they might kick her out."

"According to him," Jade said. "We only have his word for it."

Stuart shrugged. "There's the pregnancy test..."

"Which we can't find. *And* which they must have faked. Can you even do that?"

Stuart shrugged.

"He told me they hadn't even slept together. She took some sort of pact, waiting till she'd got married."

"Interesting choice, in this day and age."

"Yeah."

The two of them watched as bags of evidence were brought out of the house and taken to the CSI van. Callum Williamson was in custody in Dumbarton. His parents were staying with a relative, being watched by Colleen Glover. For now, Jade was satisfied they hadn't been involved, but she wasn't entirely convinced – and knew she needed evidence not for herself, but for a jury.

"He saying anything about why he did it?" she asked.

"Nothing. He did a hundred percent no comment interview." Stuart pulled a pad from his pocket. "But I spoke to a friend of Helen's, a young woman working at the same store as her."

"Yes?"

"She told me Helen had confided that she was scared of her brother. He had a problem with her seeing Rob. He'd signed that pact too. The family are pretty happy-clappy."

Jade felt her mouth twitch. *This isn't funny*. "Not a turn of phrase we'll be using in court."

"No. But Helen's mate, Shona, she reckoned Callum thought Helen was a sinner." He turned in his seat. "Hang on. Shona was pregnant."

"You don't reckon...?" Jade spotted Stuart's expression and smiled. "I know what you're thinking."

"Ew."

"Ew indeed." Jade shook her head. "Talk to her again. Find out if she helped."

Stuart nodded.

"So why take it out on Helen," Jade wondered aloud, "and not Rob?"

"He hadn't taken the pact. Not a sinner. And besides..."

Stuart passed her his phone, with a photo of a young man. He was at least six and a half foot tall, wearing rugby colours. He was huge.

"This is Rob?" she asked.

"It is."

"So Callum was scared to go up against a brick shithouse rugby player, but fine with battering his own sister to death."

"I reckon."

She shook her head as more bags were brought out of the house. "Not only a killer, but a coward."

CHAPTER TWENTY-TWO

"I BET Jade was well mardy with you," Petra said across the dinner table. She was in a restaurant in Glasgow with Aila, her gorgeous Aberdonian girlfriend, along with Lesley Clarke and her new wife Elsa.

Lesley raised an eyebrow. "I don't think she appreciated having a more senior officer butting in on her case."

"And Mo's old boss at that."

Lesley shrugged. "That didn't help much, either. But she's a good detective. She's building a solid case, doing it properly. They'll get their conviction."

Petra waved her hand. "That's the boring bit. It's what motivated him that interests me."

"A cult," said Aila, her Highland lilt making Petra sigh.

"I wouldn't call it a cult," Petra said. "But the whole family were part of a pretty far out church. The kids signed an abstinence pact."

Lesley leaned forward. The next table was inches from theirs and this case had been front page news in the Scottish press. "And she kept to it, DI Tanner told me. The PM showed no sexual activity."

"Poor girl," said Aila, squeezing Petra's knee under the table. Petra felt her heart flutter.

Petra's heart had never done that before. Was this a proper relationship? One that was going to last?

"Anyway, I hope it didn't ruin your honeymoon too much," she said.

"You make a lovely couple," Aila added.

Lesley and Petra exchanged glances. Elsa cupped Lesley's chin in her hand. "I think so."

Lesley flashed her eyes at Elsa.

"Och, get a room," Petra said.

Lesley turned to her. "We have. We've got one night in the Hilton, then we're heading back home."

"You've had enough of the murder-ridden Loch Lomond."

"Something like that," Elsa said.

"You do know there are more murders per capita in Glasgow than in any other part of Scotland?" Petra said.

"Not in the Hilton, though," replied Elsa.

"You'd be surprised," Lesley and Petra said in unison, then laughed.

"Some hotels have a dead room," Petra said. "A room that's used to keep bodies for a wee while before the coroner can take them."

"And you'd be surprised to know how many people die from natural causes in hotel beds," Lesley added.

"Not always all that natural, either," Petra said.

"No."

Elsa shuddered. "Let's not talk about it. I don't want to

find myself having to represent a suspected murderer while I'm here."

"You won't," Aila said. "Different legal system."

Elsa smiled at her. "Of course, you're a lawyer."

"Family law. Not criminal." Aila wrinkled her nose. "Much nicer."

"I'm not so sure," said Petra. She looked at Lesley. "So how's things in Dorset? Did they reopen the investigation into your predecessor's death?"

Lesley shook her head. "Lack of resources. Or at least that's what they said."

Elsa put a finger on Lesley's lips. "We're not talking about the MCIT while we're here."

"MCIT?" Aila asked.

"Major Crime Investigations Team," Lesley said. "And no. I've rejected half a dozen calls from my DCs while I've been here. None from my DS though, so I know I don't need to worry."

"See? I told you they'd be OK without you," Elsa said.

Lesley had a faraway look in her eye that Petra recognised. "Yes," she replied, not sounding entirely convinced.

CHAPTER TWENTY-THREE

"We've got Callum's fingerprints in Helen's blood," Jamie said. "Behind her wardrobe."

They were in the CCU offices in Glasgow, running over progress on the forensics. The entire team, bar Petra, was in the meeting room. Petra was on speakerphone, Jade's mobile in the middle of the table. The office outside was as deserted as ever.

"Nowhere else?" Jade asked.

"There's traces of bleach all over the room," he said. "He cleaned up. But he missed a spot."

"And you don't have any spatter?"

"Amazingly, no. He could have put bin bags down before he did it. There's no sign of the pack of bags containing the one he hid the hammer in."

"So it was premeditated," Mo said.

"That's not for me to judge," Jamie told him.

"I observed the video of his interview," Petra said, her voice faint. "He reacted when you mentioned the pregnancy. He was angry."

"Angry enough to kill her?" Jade asked.

"He said nothing, but he made a gesture when he was asked about it. A gripping and lifting motion. Almost imperceptible, but it was there."

"Like he would have done with the hammer," Stuart added.

"That's the one," Petra said.

Jade looked at Jamie. "How long do you think you'll be at the house?"

"That depends on budget. We've only got resource for one more day right now."

"You think you'll have everything we need by then?"

"We've checked for blood, taken anything that might yield DNA. But to be honest Jade, it looks like you've got what you need for a conviction."

"Never assume," she told him. "Keep going. We'll review what we have and if I need you to do more, I'll talk to Fraser."

Jamie looked at Stuart, making Jade frown. She and Detective Superintendent Fraser Murdo were good friends, had been while Dan was alive. But now a rumour seemed to be circulating that they were more than friends. She didn't like the insinuation that her unit was given preference because of her closeness to the Superintendent.

"The blood prints are enough for the Procurator Fiscal," said Mo, "surely?"

"That and the CCTV of him hiding the hammer," Jade said. "And the account of his relationship with his sister from her colleague. What about the car, Jamie?"

"It's at the pound in Pomaldie. We've got blood in the boot, Callum's prints on the steering wheel."

"Rob's adamant that Callum borrowed it the day Helen

was killed, and dropped it back the following morning. And he's given us a solid alibi for the night of the murder itself."

"He was at work," Stuart added. "Night shift."

"What about when we went to speak to him?"

"He was at his mum's, in Balloch."

"And the pregnancy test?"

Stuart and Mo shrugged in unison.

"Forensics haven't found it," Mo said. "No idea what happened to it."

"It might have been negative," Stuart suggested. "Maybe Callum didn't know the difference."

"Gail would have," Patty said. "And the mate, Shona, said she provided Helen with a urine sample."

Jade glanced at Stuart; he had that *ew* look on his face again.

"We'll keep looking for it," she said. "But it looks like Callum was trying to set Rob up."

"He wasn't thinking about the forensics," Jamie said.

"Then we can charge him?" Mo asked.

"We can." Jade took a breath in and put her hand on the desk. "This isn't over yet, but it's looking like this poor woman's killer will be brought to justice. Well done, everyone."

And well done, DCI Clarke, she thought but would never say aloud.

CHAPTER TWENTY-FOUR

The M8 had been clear and Lesley and Elsa were on the M74 in no time, hills passing on either side, reminding them of what they were leaving behind.

Elsa, in the driver's seat, reached across and grabbed Lesley's hand. "We'll come back. And there won't be a dead body next time."

Lesley leaned back. "That cabin was lovely. And there's lots of walking nearby."

"None of which we got to do, because you were too busy giving statements to the police."

"I'm sorry."

"I've already told you, it's OK." Elsa squeezed her hand. "Well, it's not entirely OK. I'd rather have seen more of you on our honeymoon. But I understand."

"Thanks."

Lesley had her phone on her lap. She kept turning it over. She'd promised herself she'd wait until they crossed the border before picking up messages.

"You're dying to know what's been going on, aren't you?"

Elsa asked. "You haven't stopped looking at your phone since you woke up."

"I'll check it at Gretna Green. We can stop for coffee."

"And to buy some tacky souvenirs."

Lesley smiled. "Sharon will like that."

"Go on," Elsa said. "Check them. You'll only stress about it otherwise."

"You sure?"

"I'm sure."

There were four missed calls from Stanley and three from Tina. One voicemail message, left yesterday at the same time she'd missed a call from Tina. Still nothing from Dennis, her DS and second in command.

Good old Dennis. He knew better than to disturb a woman on her honeymoon.

She picked up the message from Tina, gazing out of the window as she listened. After a few moments, she was unable to focus on the view.

"What is it?" Elsa asked. "You've turned pale."

Lesley swallowed. She can't have heard right.

She played the message again.

"Tell me, love," Elsa said. "You're worrying me."

Lesley looked at the satnav. Four hundred miles to go, still. *Damn.*

"Can you drive a bit faster, love?"

"What is it? Is it Sharon?"

"No. I spoke to Sharon yesterday." There was no ban on picking up messages from her daughter.

"Who, then?"

"It's Dennis. He's—"

"He's what?"

"Please. Let's skip the coffee stop. We need to get back."

Thank you for reading *The Lochside Murder*. You can get to know Petra, Jade and Mo in the McBride & Tanner crime series.

And you can read the next instalment in the Dorset Crime series and find out why Lesley needs to rush home in *The Lighthouse Murders*.

READ THE MCBRIDE & TANNER CRIME SERIES

Blood & Money, McBride & Tanner Book 1

Death & Poetry, McBride & Tanner Book 2

Power & Treachery, McBride & Tanner Book 3

...and more to come!

Buy now in ebook, paperback or audiobook

READ THE DORSET CRIME SERIES

...and more to come!

Buy now in ebook, paperback or audiobook

ALSO BY RACHEL MCLEAN

The DI Zoe Finch Series – Buy in ebook, paperback and audiobook

Deadly Wishes, DI Zoe Finch Book 1

Deadly Choices, DI Zoe Finch Book 2

Deadly Desires, DI Zoe Finch Book 3

Deadly Terror, DI Zoe Finch Book 4

Deadly Reprisal, DI Zoe Finch Book 5

Deadly Fallout, DI Zoe Finch Book 6

Deadly Christmas, DI Zoe Finch Book 7

Deadly Origins, the FREE Zoe Finch prequel

Made in the USA
Las Vegas, NV
23 May 2023

72461659R00059